W9-CKM-140

This Mudpie story
is for my brother,
Brad.

Published by Modern Publishing
A Division of Unisystems, Inc.

Copyright © 1978, 1980, 1987, 1988
Guy Gilchrist Productions, Inc.

MUDPIE AND HIS FAMILY™ and character names are
trademarks of Guy Gilchrist Productions, Inc.

® Honey Bear Books is a trademark owned by
Honey Bear Productions, Inc., and is registered in the
U.S. Patent and Trademark Office.

No part of this book may be reproduced or copied
without written permission from the publisher.
All Rights Reserved.

Printed in Spain

Mudpie's Island Adventure

by Guy Gilchrist

MODERN PUBLISHING
A Division of Unisystems, Inc.
New York, N.Y. 10022

Hi! My name is Mudpie. My sister Punkin and my pal Trapper are not very happy today. It's raining outside, so we can't go out to play.

Punkin says there's nothing to do indoors, but I told her there's lots to do if we just use our imaginations.

We closed our eyes and made a dream-wish.

We dream-wished for my bedroom walls to turn into a blue sky and for my floor to become a big, warm ocean.

All of a sudden, we were sailing away in the middle of the ocean, surrounded by funny colored birds and checkerboard dolphins.

"Land ho!" I shouted as I sailed our ship to the shore of Dream Wish Island.

We started to explore and discovered the most amazing things!

Punkin saw a kangaroo that hopped upside down.
Everytime she jumped, her stuff fell out of her pocket.

I found a tree that grew peanut butter and jelly sandwiches, so I climbed to the top and ate as many as I wanted to.

But then the peanut butter and jelly monkeys found me, and chased me out of their tree!

I ran to our ship and sailed away over the ocean and past the clouds . . .

all the way back to my bedroom.

Then my mom came in and said naptime was over
and that it had stopped raining while we were asleep.

"ASLEEP!" I shouted. "We weren't sleeping. We were on an island adventure!"

"Of course you were," my mom said. "Now come into the kitchen, kids. It's time for lunch."

We had peanut butter and jelly sandwiches. I took mine outside and ate it up in a tree.